DEMAIN PUBLISHING

<u>Short Sharp Shocks!</u>

Book 0: Dirty Paws - Dean M. Drinkel
Book 1: Patient K - Barbie Wilde
Book 2: The Stranger & The Ribbon – Tim Dry
Book 3: Asylum Of Shadows – Stephanie Ellis
Book 4: Monster Beach – Ritchie Valentine Smith
Book 5: Beasties & Other Stories – Martin Richmond
Book 6: Every Moon Atrocious – Emile-Louis Tomas Jouvet
Book 7: A Monster Met – Liz Tuckwell
Book 8: The Intruders & Other Stories – Jason D. Brawn
Book 9: The Other – David Youngquist
Book 10: Symphony Of Blood – Leah Crowley
Book 11: Shattered – Anthony Watson
Book 12: The Devil's Portion – Benedict J. Jones
Book 13: Cinders Of A Blind Man Who Could See – Kev Harrison
Book 14: Dulce Et Decorum Est – Dan Howarth
Book 15: Blood, Bears & Dolls – Allison Weir
Book 16: The Forest Is Hungry – Chris Stanley
Book 17: The Town That Feared Dusk – Calvin Demmer
Book 18: Night Of The Rider – Alyson Faye
Book 19: Isidora's Pawn – Erik Hofstatter
Book 20: Plain – D.T. Griffith
Book 21: Supermassive Black Mass – Matthew Davis

Book 46: The Birthday Girl & Other Stories –
        Christopher Beck
Book 47: Crowded House & Other Stories - S.J.
        Budd
Book 48: Hand To Mouth – Deborah Sheldon
Book 49: Moonlight Gunshot Mallet Flame / A
        Little Death – Alicia Hilton
Book 50: Dark Corners - David Charlesworth

Murder! Mystery! Mayhem!

Maggie Of My Heart – Alyson Faye
The Funeral Birds – Paula R.C. Readman
Cursed – Paul M. Feeney
The Bone Factory – Yolanda Sfetsos
Garland Cove – Deborah Sheldon
Death In The Dugout – Bruce Harris

Beats! Ballads! Blank Verse!

Book 1: Echoes From An Expired Earth – Allen
Ashley
Book 2: Grave Goods – Cardinal Cox
Book 3: From Long Ago – Paul Woodward
Book 4: Laws Of Discord – William Clunie
Book 5: Fanged Dandelion – Eric LaRocca

Weird! Wonderful! Other Worlds

Book 1: The Raven King – Liz Tuckwell
Book 2: The Wired City – Yolanda Sfetsos

Horror Novels & Novellas

House Of Wrax – Raven Dane
And Blood Did Fall – Chad A. Clark

The Underclass – Dan Weatherer
Cheslyn Myre – Dan Weatherer
Greenbeard – John Travis
Tower Of Raven – Kevin M. Folliard
Little Bird – TR Hitchman
Society Place – Andrew David Barker

The 'A QUIET APOCALYPSE' Series

A Quiet Apocalypse – Dave Jeffery
Cathedral (A Quiet Apocalypse Book 2) – Dave Jeffery
The Samaritan (A Quiet Apocalypse Book 3) – Dave Jeffery
A Silent Dystopia – Edited by D.T. Griffith

General Fiction

Joe – Terry Grimwood
Finding Jericho – Dave Jeffery

Science Fiction Collections

Vistas – Chris Kelso

Horror Fiction Collections

Distant Frequencies – Frank Duffy
Where We Live – Tim Cooke
Night Voices – Paul Edwards & Frank Duffy

Anthologies

The Darkest Battlefield – Tales Of WW1/Horror

THE CORN WITCH

BY
CHRISTOPHER BECK

A SHORT! SHARP! SHOCKS! BOOK

BOOK 63

For further information, please visit:
WEB: www.demainpublishing.com
TWITTER: @DemainPubUk
FACEBOOK: Demain Publishing
INSTAGRAM: demainpublishing

For William Connolly
"I did it!"

CONTENTS

THE CORN WITCH

As the dying sun disappears, leaving its bloody mark on the Western sky, the chocolate lab crawls from the hollow tree stump. He yawns and stretches his haunches, then sniffs the evening air. A hundred scents pass through his olfactory receptors but he is only interested in those that lead to food.

He looks back at the place he's come to know as home. He cannot remember much of the previous one just that it was much nicer, warmer, and that he didn't have to scrounge for food or sleep in the dirt.

His sunken stomach rumbles and aches. He sniffs the air again; there's nothing in the immediate area to help with the hunger pains. He chooses a direction and walks along sniffing at the ground.

It's easier at night, he has learned, to look for food: there isn't anyone yelling or kicking at him, or taking a shot; there are no vehicles on the road to dodge should he need to cross it. Yes, night is better.

He picks up a fresh scent but it's one that doesn't smell too good. It's familiar, however, and he remembers once chasing something through the brush that ended up spraying him with something that stung his eyes and nose and left him stinking for weeks.

He presses on, sniffing for something more favorable.

He kicks up a small and furry creature that quickly scurries away from him. He can smell its fear and it smells delicious.

If he wasn't starved he would have prolonged the hunt, enjoyed a little cat-and-mouse, if you will. But he doesn't have the energy for such a game, and he can't risk a meal getting away.

He pins his struggling prey down with his front paws and goes in for a bite.

Hey pup.

He looks up, wondering where it came from.

That's right. Come here, pup.

Despite the extreme hunger, he releases the small creature.

That's a good boy.

His ears twitch, trying to find the source. He walks forward and the trees give way, the land before him is flat and empty. He looks and sniffs.

So close. Come on now.

He takes a step forward but then steps back.

Don't be afraid.

Nose in the air, he takes a step forward.

That's it.

He turns his nose to the ground, takes another step.

Almost there.

He steps out of the woods and yelps as something bursts through the ground and grabs him. He bucks and snarls, trying to break free. He almost succeeds.

Such a good boy.

***

A late-summer wind comes with the resurrection of the sun and Monica, sipping her coffee at the kitchen counter, watches as it blows the Red Maple around. The front lawn is on the small side but the tree is one of her favorite things about the new house. She breaths deep and smiles, lets out a satisfied sigh. She feels good about the move.

Adam comes into the kitchen and wraps an arm around her waist. Her smile widens. She places a hand on his forearm and leans her head back into his shoulder, which she kisses.

He kisses the back of her neck. "Good morning."

"Moring, baby," she says.

"So what do you think?"

She cranes her head back. "It's growing on me."

They both smile and their lips meet. Then their tongues. She can feel him growing hard and reaches back to rub his bulge. She moans. His hands cup her breasts as he kisses her neck. Her hand reaches around his neck and rubs his head.

Footsteps upstairs pause their primal lust. They listen as the steps pad into the upstairs bathroom. After a moment the toilet flushes and the shower starts.

Monica shoves her pajama bottoms and underwear down around her ankles and leans forward on the counter. "Make it quick."

"Yes, ma'am," Adam says.

***

Pete wasn't in favor of the move to 613 Richard's Road. He didn't have many friends and the few he left behind were very dear: Tom he had known since pre-school. They befriended Henry and Josh in middle school and together they all had played D&D, snuck liquor from their parents' cabinets, masturbated over used Playboy mags. How was he going to find such friends here in Upper Deerfield, New Jersey? This morning, however, a week after the fact, he seems closer to his old cheery self.

"Good morning."

"Morning."

"Good Morning, squirt."

Pete grabs a bowl from their new cabinet and the rest of the parts needed for his cereal breakfast. In the nook he makes a mess upon the table as he adds too much cereal followed by too much milk.

"Can I go fly my kite?" He says between crunches.

"Have you unpacked all of your boxes?" Monica says.

"Yes."

"Oh, yeah?"

Pete hesitates, furrows his brow and frowns. "No. I still have my box of books..."

"And?" Adam says.

"And a box of clothes...but I'll take care of them, I promise."

"Today?" Monica says.

"Yes! I promise!"

Adam gives Monica a look that say he's ready for another round and she gives him a knowing smile in return.

"All right," she says. "You can go fly your kite as long as you take care of those boxes before bed tonight."

Pete beamed. "I will! Promise!"

"And," Adam adds. "You have to clean up your mess there."

Pete nods as he shovels the last spoonful of cereal into his mouth.

***

The flesh and blood of the stray dog is a miserable form of sustenance but one needed to keep her energy from completely fading. The cool and damp earth is heavy on her. She's used to its weight, has often been comforted by it, but she's been confined for far too long. She doesn't know years or months or even days and therefore doesn't know, in those terms, how long she's been trapped here. To her it feels like eons. It was the corn and the fear that grew with it that used draw her from hibernation, but those above ground stopped sowing the field. They thought that would keep her at bay but they didn't account for the cobs and kernels that were left behind, some mushed down into the soil, ready for the next season. The size of the crop grew smaller, sure, but that was of no matter: as long as there were stalks, there would be fear. Then those above, living near the field, all went away and the fear was gone. The brief fear of the stray and wild animals she's used to keep her energy alive is worth little.

***

Pete smiles as his kite dances in the blue sky. His aunt Jenny gifted him his first kite on his 8th birthday and had found new and exciting ones to wrap up for him each of the five birthdays since.

He glances across the street, past the Red Maple, at the small kitchen window. His mom had told him to stay in sight of said window but, because of the closed curtains, he cannot tell if she's watching from the other side.

A gust comes along and takes his kite higher. Pete lets out some more string and wonders how high his kite will fly today. Hopefully the highest it's ever gone!

A car passes and he glances back at the road. There is no wave or beep from the blue sedan but he waves anyway. In the week that they have been here, he's come to learn that their little road doesn't see much travel at all. He had wondered what his dad had meant by sleepy little town but now he think her knows the answer.

The kite dips and Pete steps forward and wheels some of the string in. Once the kite is settled it its flight again he looks back across the road.

There are three other houses along the strip of macadam: one to the left of the new home, two to the right.

The two on the right have bright and colorful 'For Sale' signs sitting along the edge of manicured lawns, but the one on the left, well, the lawn there looks as if it hasn't been attended to in months: the grass, filled with dandelions, is knee high, the round shrubs along the front walk are also wildly over grown, weeds stand tall in the flower garden, and ivy cover most of the wall to the left of the front door.

To the right, streaked with filth, is a bay window, standing in it is an older man. The man is tall and thin with grey stubble and a headful of unkempt gray hair.

Pete once again raises his hand but, like the driver, the old man doesn't return his wave. He just stands there, unmoving. It's creepy, and Pete finds himself backing further from the road and closer to the woods. He stops only when he can no longer see the features of the old man.

The kite dips and Pete quickly takes in the slack and pulls the string tight again. The kite settles in the sky, Pete looks to the left and the right trying to guesstimate the size of the field.

"Wonder what they used to plant here?"

It was corn.

The unexpected response caused Pete's breath to catch and his heart to skip a beat. He almost let the spool be pulled from his hands.

"Who said that?" His head swiveled in every direction but there was no one around.

I did.

The voice low and even. Feminine. Welcoming.

Pete turned and studied the woods, looking for a form crouching next to a shrub or standing just behind a tree.

"I see you! Why are you hiding there?"

I'm not hiding anywhere.

Pete points. "You're right by that tree!"

Silly boy. I'm not by any tree. The woods isn't a place for a lady such as me.

Pete, again, looks all around. The silhouette of the old man is still framed by the dirty bay window but there is no one nearby.

"Where are you then?"

I am beneath you.

Pete didn't look down but around again.

"What do you mean?"

Beneath you, silly boy. Beneath the field.

The kite dips and then pulls again but Pete doesn't register the movement. Eyes wide, mouth wide, he stares down at his feet.

"Beneath? How, why, how can...who are you?"

That is an excellent question. But, before I answer, may I have the pleasure of your name?

"P...Pete. It's Pete."

It's a pleasure, Pete. I am Mae. Better known as the corn witch.

"The Corn Witch?"

The one and only, at least around here.

Pete licks his lips with a dry tongue. He feels the need to reel in his kite, head on into the house, but, despite his tepidness, he was also curious. He said the first thing that came to mind.

"But there's no corn."

Sadly, Pete, this field has been forgotten.

"By the farmers? Why?"

By everyone. A long time ago this was barren land, meaning it wasn't good for planting. Those stubborn enough to stay and attempt to settle this land, in time, became desperate. None of their crops took, and the wildlife could only last so long. They needed SOMETHING to survive and that something was me.

"How did..."

That's not important. What is important is that life returns to this field; what is important is that I am not forgotten. Would you care to help me with that?

Pete doesn't know what to say and says what seems to be the only logical answer. "Ah...sure..."

Excellent!

"What do, ah, do you need me to do?"

Pete wants to take the words back as soon as they leave his mouth.

Another Great question, Pete! What I need is for you to fear me.

"Wait...what...?"

Turn around.

Pete swallows hard. His hands are clammy and his heart is thundering. Slowly he turns around and gasps.

Standing directly behind him is the dog, its head lowered as if sniffing the ground, but its milky white eyes are staring right him. Large patches of flesh have been torn from the stray and the exposed portions of skeleton are still wet with blood.

Pete screams.

The dog's mouth moves as if speaking.

See you soon.

The dog collapses.

Pete breathes and screams again. He lets the spool go and his kite takes off across the sky. He trips on his own feet as he turns to run home. A rock bites into his knee. The ground sinks beneath his hands. Tears burn his eyes. He wipes them away and sees a pair of legs before him. He looks up and sees the old man from next door.

The old man grunts and holds out a hand.

***

Pete sits in a kitchen chair attempting to tell the story between ragged breaths. Monica is cleaning the wound on his knee. Adam is standing just behind her. The old man leans back against the front door, arms crossed.

"Slow down," Adam says. "Breathe."

"Thank you for bringing him home." Monica says looking up at the old man.

"Yes. Thank you." Adam says. He steps forward and offers his hand. "What's your name?" He looks at his son. "And what happened?"

The old man ignores Adam's gesture. "What happened was that you two were too busy fucking like jack rabbits to pay attention to your son."

Monica's face flushes red.

Before Adam can respond, the old man points to side window facing his house. "You forgot to close those curtains."

"You were watching us?" Adam spat. "Who the hell do you think you are?"

"No. I only noticed. I was watching your son."

"And why the fuck were you watching our son?"

"Because you weren't; and because of her."

Adam looks at his wife and then back at the old man. He points at Monica. "You mean her?"

"No." The old man says. "I mean the corn witch."

"What the fuck are you talking about?" Adam says. His eyes are filled with fire. He takes another step forward and is nose to nose with the old man. "You're fucking crazy. First you watch me and my wife through the window and now you're talking about some witch? Look at my son. Did you do this to him?"

Adam turns to Pete. "Did he hurt you?"

Pete, tears still streaming down his cheeks, shakes his head.

"What's your angle old man?"

"Ain't no angle but her," he hooks a thumb over his shoulder, "and you all are going to find that out real soon."

"Get the fuck out of my house." Adam says.

"Now," Monica says. She's standing now, with cell phone in hand. "Before I call the cops."

The old man grunts before turning to open the door. As he steps outside he can hear Pete say, "He's telling the truth."

***

Pete falls asleep listening to his parents whisper about him and is suspended in complete darkness. He reaches out his hands and his feet but feels nothing.

"Hello?"

See you soon.

In a cold sweat Pete shoots up in his bed. Wide eyed he looks in every corner of his bedroom: the street light provides just enough light for him to see he's alone. He sighs and slumps back onto his bed; calms his breathing.

He doesn't think sleep again is possible but after a while his heavy eyelids are falling shut. He fights to keep them open but soon loses the battle.

There is no darkness this time. Just himself, in bed, lightly snoring.

And a light scraping upon the window.

The sound doesn't disturb him at first but as the wind pickups the scraping becomes more frequent. Louder.

Pete turns over and tries to ignore it.

The sound intensifies.

Pete sighs, wondering what could be causing it, then realizes his bedroom is on the second floor, far from any trees.

His eyes fly open and stare at the wall. He doesn't want to lift his head from the pillow but knows he has to.

He pushes himself up and looks toward the window opposite the foot of his bed.

Corn stalks.

Of course, standing thick and full before his window, their green leaves finding purchase on the doubled paned glass.

Scared yet curious, Pete throws back the covers. As his bare feet touch the cool floor, a chill touches his skin. He tries to rub the bumps away as he tentatively approaches the window. There's something hypnotic about the way the stalks sway.

Pete touches the glass. He feels the need to touch the waving leaves but refuses to open the window.

The wind stops, the stalks and their leaves become still. There's a silence deeper than Pete has ever heard. A moment passes then the stalks split straight down the middle, offering him a view of the empty field.

The mutilated dog is there, just on the other side of the road, sitting on its back haunches looking up at his window.

The chill on Pete's skin becomes a shiver down his spine.

Fear me.

The corn stalks rush back together violently.

Pete gasps and stumbles away from the window. His bed catches him just below the knees and he falls backward.

When he wakes again it's to chirping birds and a bright morning sun. Pete rubs the sleep from his still tired eyes and sits up on the edge of the bed. From down the hall comes a giggle from his mother and the faint sound of squeaky bed springs. Pete groans in disgust.

He stands and walks to the window. It both repels and compels him and he knows there is no choice but to look out at the field.

There is no dog, thank god, but the old man is there, staring at a patch of short green stalks.

Pete rubs his eyes again and takes another look. The stalks are indeed there. He quickly changes out of his pajamas, slips on his socks and shoes, and sneaks down the stairs and out the front door.

The old man nods at him as he approaches and Pete, unsure of what to say, nods back.

"Your folks see this yet?"

Pete shakes his head. "No. They are, uh, still in bed."

"Course they are."

"She's real, isn't she?"

"As real as you and me." The old man points with the toe of his boot. "As real as these stalks."

Pete looks up at the old man. "How do you know about her?"

That's not important. He's an old toy and he cannot help you, despite all of his bravado.

"Can you hear her?"

The old man gives a quick shake of his head. "And I don't want to know what she's saying. Our paths will cross again soon enough, and I'll be ready."

Pete, can you hear it? He's scared! I haven't felt fear from this one in many moons.

The ground around the old man erupts. Tall, thick stalks shoot up around him, erasing him from Pete's view. Pete tries to scream but is temporarily paralyzed. The old man does scream as the long, thin leaves on the stalks turn red.

Oh, thank you, Pete.

Pete pisses himself, the warmth of which thaws some of the ice holding him in place. He finds his voice as he runs for the house. Behind him he can hear fresh corn stalks bursting from the ground.

***

The harvest of the old man is a welcomed surprised as it's happened far sooner than she anticipated. He had stopped fearing her long ago, but fear never truly dies: like the soil around her, it just lies dormant until a fresh seed is planted.

And the boy: his fear is greater than she could have hoped for. She smiles, proud of herself. Tonight, she thinks. Tonight I will taste the sky once again.

***

"How is this possible?" Monica says.

The three of them are standing on the edge of the front lawn staring over the macadam at the tall and healthy corn stalks that now take up nearly half of the field.

"I...don't know," Adam says. "But there's no way corn stalks ate our neighbor."

"I'm not making it up, Dad, you have to call..."

"Enough, Pete. I don't what's going with you and these corn witch stories— maybe you had a nightmare or, god forbid, a hallucination—but I do know that plants don't kill people and that crazy old man started all of this with his damn fairytale."

"But Dad…"

"No buts. We're going to settle this bullshit once and for all." Adam turns and makes for the old man's house. "Come on."

They skirt around the tall grass and snake their way up the front walk, weaving between the branches of the overgrown shrubs.

Monica groans in disgust. "How can anyone live like this?"

"I don't know," Adam says. "And right now I don't care."

Pete, nerves still tingling, tears still washing his face, wants to scream at his parents, wants to finally grab their attention and make them understand that the state of the old man's landscaping is the least of their worries, and that they are not going to find him inside the house, but says nothing.

Adam pounds on the door with the side of his fist causing the window next to it to rattle in its frame.

"Open up, old man."

Without waiting for a response he pounds on the door again.

"Enough fucking around. Open the door."

This time Adam does wait a moment, but his brow and his anger deepen when there is no response. He hammers the door harder and longer.

"Calm down, hunny."

"I'll calm down when this crazy old fuck opens the door. I know you're in there!"

"Dad, he isn't in there."

Adam ignores the comment. He stops hammering and reaches for the doorknob. "If you don't want to come out, then we'll come in."

"Adam, no..."

The door isn't locked and it opens onto a small living room. Like the lawn behind them the room is in disarray. Stale cigarette smoke clings to the air. The carpet is dirty and stained, littered with soiled clothes, used paper plates and cups. The coffee table hosts a number of overfilled ashtrays, an old pipe, several cigarette packs, and a box of wooden matches. The saggy couch against the far wall is covered with notebooks, loose leaf paper, and newspapers. Hanging above it on the wall is a doubled headed axe. Next to the old Laz-y-boy in the corner, leaning against the wall, is a shotgun. Sitting on the other side of the chair are two five gallon gas cans.

"What the hell?" Adam says.

Monica pulls on his arm. "We should go."

"In a second. Stay here."

"Adam, don't…"

Tentatively Adam steps into the house. "Uh, hello?" All the bass has left his voice. To his left is the kitchen, he starts his search there.

Monica stays on the front step but Pete does not. He's drawn to the couch and the papers on it.

The newspapers have yellowed and display years that predate the births of both his parents. Each of them feature, in different lengths, stories about the field and the corn witch. The notebooks appear to be journals of the old man's history with the witch, and the loose papers are filled with notes about Pete and his family.

"Mom, Dad, look! I told you he was telling the truth."

"What are you doing?" Adam says as he returns to the living room. "I told you to wait outside."

"I don't like this," Monica says. "We should leave, now."

Pete raises up one of the newspapers. "Look at the headline, it says 'Corn Witch Returns'."

"Put that down and let's go."

"Why won't you listen to me?"

"Because I've heard enough of this bullshit."

Pete points at the other newspapers. "How can all of this be bullshit?"

"Watch your mouth, young man." Monica says.

"I'm not telling you again. Let's go."

Defeated again, Pete sets the newspaper back down. He wants to scoop up all of the stories, all of the notes, take them home and study them line by line. Surely there's something within all those pages that would finally convince his parents that the old man wasn't crazy. He sighs and follows his parents back home.

***

The light squeak of his bedroom window raising in its frame is what wakes Pete. As the humid night air drifts in around him, he stares at his door. It's closed and helps to muffle the voices of his parents coming from downstairs. A long shadow covers him and he bites his lip to keep from screaming.

I know you are awake.

Fresh hot tears burn Pete's eyes. He bites down harder drawing blood.

Look at me.

Pete squeezes his eyes. Shakes his head.

And here I thought we were becoming friends.

"Please go away," Pete ekes out.

You know I can't do that. Now look at me, or I will tear the eyelids from your face.

Pete chokes out a sob. A mix of blood and saliva floes over his bottom lip and drips down on his pillow. He struggles to find his next breath. The sound of fear swimming in his ears is deafening. "O...oh...okay."

Over the past couple of days his imagination has conjured up many images of the corn witch, none of which were even close to the thing floating at the foot of his bed.

Hello, Pete.

The corn witch smiles, exposing diseased gums and a handful of rotten teeth. Her eyes are the color of dark piss with black pinpricks for pupils. Dark, bushy eyebrows hood her eyes; dark, greasy hair hangs down around her shoulders. A long and crooked nose protrudes from her bulbous face; exposed pendulous breasts hang down in front of her large stomach. Her flesh is smeared with dirt. Where her legs should be is a green and tapered tail.

Pete watches in horror as the tail reaches out toward him. The tip splits in to four parts. The four parts stretch out like deformed fingers and take hold of his ankle.

This is where you scream.

Pete does so.

Confused gasps come from downstairs followed by heavy footsteps on the stairs.

The corn witch cackles as the bedroom door flies open.

Do you believe your son now?

She pulls Pete from the bed (the sudden collision with the floor interrupts his screaming) and floats toward the open window dragging him behind her.

Pete claws at the floor, trying to find purchase on the carpet. His free foot meets the wall below the window and he tries to shove off of it.

"Mom! Dad!"

Adam lunges forward and grabs a hold of Pete's hands. He grinds down his heels but the witch is much stronger and he too is pulled off his feet, toward the open window.

"Monica. The bat."

Peeking out from under Pete's bed is his bat and glove.

Without a second thought Monica snatches up the bat and brings it down hard the witch's tail.

"Let go of my son!"

The witch staggers in the air. Adam draws up on his knees and pulls again. Pete slides forward as he moves backwards. Monica slams the bat home again, and again. The witch yelps and finally releases Pete.

Monica slams the window shut, watches the witch dive back into the corn.

Adam pulls Pete to him, hugs him hard.

Monica drops to her knees and joins the embrace.

"She'll be back," Pete says.

***

There's no skirting the high grass this time, they cut right through it and quickly enter the old man's house.

Adam snatches up the shotgun. It takes a few moments but he quickly figures out how to break it open: both barrels have bright red shells in them. He snaps it shut again and thumbs what he believes is the safety.

Monica steps up on the couch, removes the axe; it's heavy in her hands.

Pete stands behind them both, staring out the bay window. The corn stalks dance on the wind; the corn witch dances above them, her tail reaching down every so often and then curving up to her mouth.

"She has strength again but she isn't strong as she hopes to be."

Both Adam and Monica start to ask Pete how he knows this but remember how they doubted him and cut their questions short.

Adam looks down at Pete, places a hand on his shoulder. "I don't know how any of this shit is possible, but I am sorry that I didn't believe you."

Monica touches his other shoulder. "I'm sorry, too."

Before they can hug again, something crashes through the bay window and slams down on the floor.

It is what is left of the old man.

Pete turns his head and backs up against the wall, bile rising in the back of his throat.

Monica screams.

Adam takes the Lord's name in vain.

I can smell your fear. And it smells glorious!

"Where are you?" Adam says.

I am everywhere.

"You're full of shit!" Pete says.

Pete. I'm impressed by your resolve. But it's your fear I love most.

"Then come and get me you bitch."

Oh, Pete. Have you not yet learned that I need you alive? Someone has to tell this story, and the young most certainly spread fear faster than the old. The question now is which of your parents do I eat first?

Monica goes to the broken window. "Why don't you start with me?"

Adam starts to protest but Monica mouths to him, "Be ready."

The corn witch once again takes center stage and stares back at Monica.

It would be my pleasure.

She swoops down from the sky.

Monica feels her bladder loosen but doesn't move. "She's coming."

As the witch closes in on the window her tail unfurls, launching something that will make it there before her.

The thing comes quick and Monica leaps to the right, losing hold of the axe.

Adam, double-barrel at the ready, pulls the trigger. The force of the explosion nearly knocks him off his feet.

The carcass of the dog misses that of the old man, slams down on the floor and slides toward Pete.

The corn witch rushes through the window knocking Adam against the wall. She circles the room, offering Pete a wink, and hovers over Monica. Her tail splits and grabs Monica by her throat.

Monica kicks and flails.

That's it, struggle.

The witch's tail splits again and the new members take hold of Monica's limbs. She leans forward and breaths deep.

Your fear smells exquisite. I cannot wait to taste it.

She inhales again.

Wait...can it be? Yes, indeed. She looks at Pete. *This changes things.*

"Let her go!" Adam roars as he bashes the butt of the gun against the corn witch's head. She falls to the floor and Adam whacks her again. She falls to her hands and knees, spitting out blackened teeth.

Monica stumbles up to her feet, takes up the axe, raises it overhead.

"Eat this you bitch!"

The blade sinks deep into the corn witch's neck. She screams as green blood sprays the floor. She tries to rise but cannot. She collapses and gurgles her last breath.

"We need to burn her," Pete says. He points at the gas cans. "And the corn."

***

Adam sets the newspaper down and reaches for his cup of coffee. "They're saying Henry set fire to the field and then to his house with himself, and his dog in it. Given his priors and checkered history, no one is really batting an eyelash."

"I wish I could've known him better." Pete says as he flips the yellowed newspaper closed.

"Me, too," Monica says.

***

Fire hurts, but fire can also cleanse. Fire can bring death but it can also bring forth new life.

***

It was a great struggle to crawl across the road to the half of field that wasn't burning, but diving deep into the soil is a great comfort. It will take time to heal, but the echo of the heartbeat she heard within the woman will give her strength.

BIOGRAPHY

Born in California but raised in New Jersey, Christopher, the author of *The Birthday Girl & Other Stories*, as well as numerous other short stories, enjoys spending his free time hiking and searching for ancient evils.

ADRIAN BALDWIN (COVER ARTIST)

Adrian is a Mancunian now living and working in Wales. Back in the 1990s, he wrote for various TV shows/personalities: Smith & Jones, Clive Anderson, Brian Conley, Paul McKenna, Hale & Pace, Rory Bremner (and a few others). Wooo, get him! Since then, he has written three screenplays—one of which received generous financial backing from the Film Agency for Wales. Then along came the global recession which kicked the UK Film industry in the nuts. What a bummer! Not to be outdone, he turned to novel writing—which had always been his real dream—and, in particular, a genre he feels is often overlooked; a genre he has always been a fan of: Dark Comedy (sometimes referred to as Horror's weird cousin). *Barnacle Brat* (a dark comedy for grown-ups), his first novel won Indie Novel of the Year 2016 award; his second novel *Stanley Mccloud Must Die!* (more dark comedy for grown-ups) published in 2016 and his third: *The Snowman And The Scarecrow* (another dark comedy for grown-ups) published in 2018. Adrian Baldwin has also written and published a number of dark comedy short stories. He designs book covers too—not just for his own books but for a growing number of publishers. For more information on the award-winning author, check out:

https://adrianbaldwin.info/

DEMAIN PUBLISHING

To keep up to-date on all news DEMAIN (including future submission calls and releases) you can follow us in a number of ways:

BLOG:
www.demainpublishingblog.weebly.com

TWITTER:
@DemainPubUk

FACEBOOK PAGE:
Demain Publishing

INSTAGRAM:
demainpublishing

www.ingramcontent.com/pod-product-compliance
Lightning Source LLC
Chambersburg PA
CBHW031514150726
47990CB00007B/3023